HODDER AND STOUGHTON
LONDON SYDNEY AUCKLAND TORONTO

Eric Carle's ANIMALS ANIMALS

For Martha and Leighton

There is only one horse on all the earth
and his name is All Horses.
There is only one bird in the air
and his name is All Wings.
There is only one fish in the seas
and his name is All Fins.
There is only one man in all the world
and his name is All Men.
There is only one woman in all the world
and her name is All Women.
There is only one child in the world
and the child's name is All Children.
There is only one Maker in all the world
and His children cover the earth,
and they are named All God's Children.

Carl Sandburg

And God created great whales, and every living creature that moveth,
which the waters brought forth abundantly after their kind . . .

Bible, Genesis

I throw myself to the left.
I turn myself to the right.
I am the fish
Who glides in the water, who glides,
Who twists himself, who leaps.
Everything lives, everything dances, everything sings.

African Pygmy

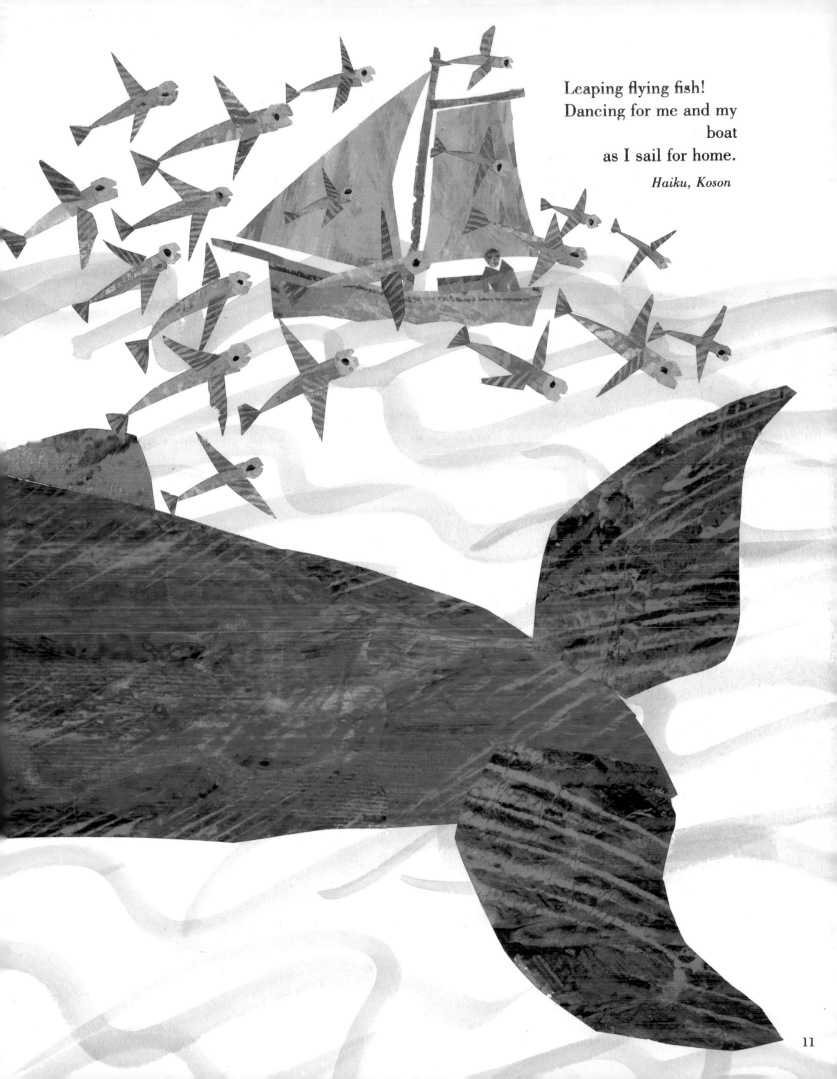

Leaping flying fish!
Dancing for me and my
boat
as I sail for home.

Haiku, Koson

11

Butterflies dancing through falling snow!
What a wonderful sight it would be!

Haiku, Demaru

How sadly the bird in his cage
Watches the butterflies.

Haiku, Issa

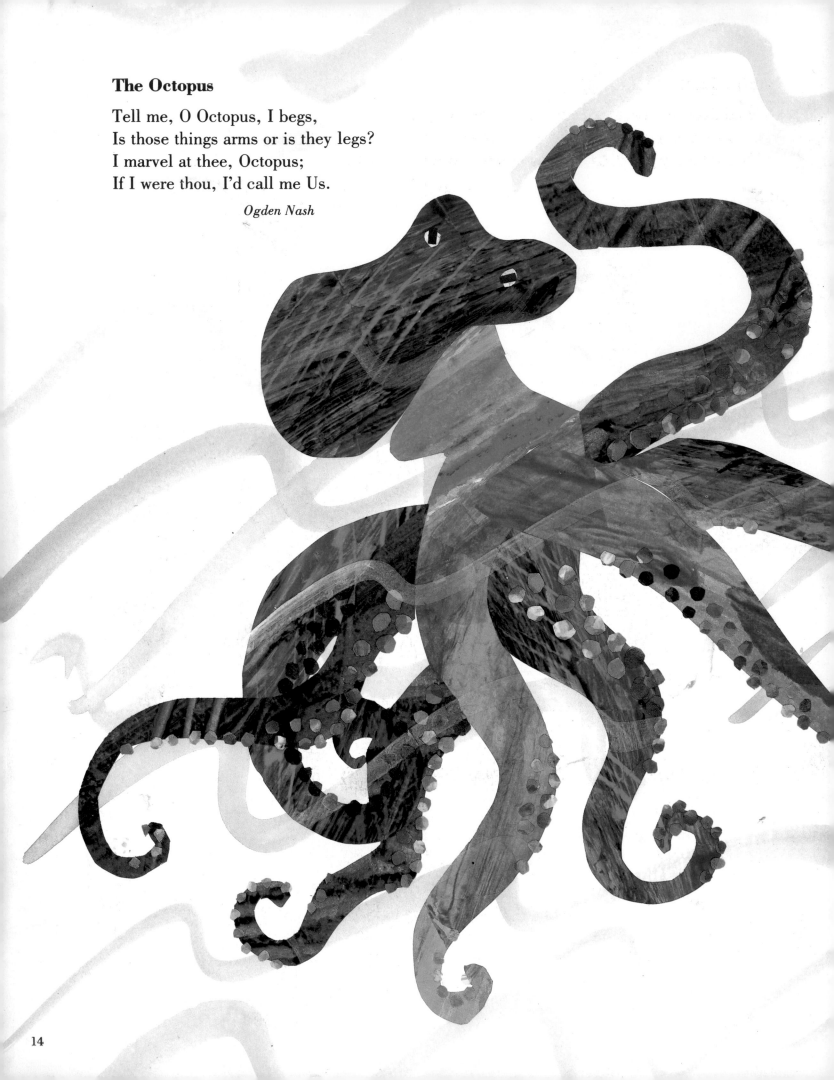

The Octopus

Tell me, O Octopus, I begs,
Is those things arms or is they legs?
I marvel at thee, Octopus;
If I were thou, I'd call me Us.

Ogden Nash

14

Sea Turtle

Paddling, we saw that turtle; saw its eyes open,
   its flippers outstretched, as it floated
Seawater lapped at its shell, spreading across its back.

Australian Aborigine

Bat

Dark air-life looping
Yet missing the pure loop . . .
A twitch, a twitter, an elastic shudder in flight
And serrated wings against the sky,
like a glove, a black glove thrown up at the light,
And falling back.

D.H. Lawrence

Every Insect

Every Insect (ant, fly, bee)
Is divided into three:
One head, one chest, one stomach part.

Some have brains.
All have a heart.

Insects have no bones,

No noses.

But with feelers they can smell
Dinner half a mile away.

Can your nose do half as well?

Also you'd be in a fix
With all those legs to manage:
Six.

Dorothy Aldis

The Ant

The ant is knowing and wise; but
he doesn't know enough to take a vacation.

Clarence Day

Crickets

We cannot say that crickets sing
Since all they do is twang a wing.

Especially when the wind is still
They orchestrate a sunlit hill.

And in the evening blue above
They weave the stars and moon with love.

Then peacefully they chirp all night
Remembering delight, delight . . .

Harry Behn

Bee! I'm Expecting You

Bee! I'm expecting you!
Was saying Yesterday
To Somebody you know
That you were due—

The Frogs got Home last Week—
And settled, and at work—
Birds, mostly back—
The Clover warm and thick—

You'll get my Letter by
The seventeenth; Reply,
Or better, be with me—
Yours, Fly.

Emily Dickinson

My Opinion

Is a caterpillar ticklish?
    Well, it's always my belief
That he giggles as he wiggles
    Across a hairy leaf.

Monica Shannon

M was once a little mouse.
    Mousy,
      Bousy,
      Sousy,
      Mousy.
In the housy,
      Little mouse!

Edward Lear

The Birthday Cow

Happy Mooday to you,
Happy Mooday to you.
Happy Mooday,
Dear Yooday.
Happy Mooday to you.

Eve Merriam

Baby Chick

Peck
   peck
     peck
on the warm brown egg.
OUT comes a neck.
OUT comes a leg.

How
   does
     a chick
who's not been about,
discover the trick
of how to get out?

Aileen Fisher

21

Commissariat Camels

We haven't a camelty tune of our own
To help us trollop along.
But every neck is a hairy trombone,
Rtt-ta-ta-ta! is a hairy trombone.
And this is our marching song:
Can't! Don't! Shan't! Won't!
Pass it along the line!

Rudyard Kipling

The bear stands.
I am telling you this.
Yonder the bear stands.
He faces the east just before the sun appears.
Yonder the bear stands.
Now the sun is coming.

Pawnee Indian

The tail of a fox will show no matter how hard he tries to hide it.

Hungarian proverb

The Duck-Billed Platypus

The duck-billed platypus isn't easy to imagine,
of all the earthly creatures he is most unique,
lays eggs like a bird but suckles like an animal,
and swims like a fish at the bottom of a creek.

If you ask it why it behaves so confusingly,
It hides in a hole and simply will not speak,
All that I can say, it's a shy individual,
An oddity of nature and a very charming freak!

Arnold Sundgaard

A Cat May Look at a King

The Cat
  Came and sat
  Down before His Majesty.
The Cat
Came and sat
Down before the King.
"I've come to take a look.
For unless I am mistook,
It is written in this book,
I may do this thing!"

She took
Quite a look.
  Over all His Majesty.
She took
Quite a look
  And then she shook her head.
"There's little here to praise.
Plain his looks and dull his ways;
I'll turn my loving gaze
On Tabby Tom instead!"

Laura Richards

28

A handful does not satisfy a lion.

Talmud

The Elephant

The elephant is quite a beast,
He's rather large to say the least,
And though his size is most impressive
The elephant is not aggressive,
He never throws his weight around,
Still he always holds his ground.
He only wants to feel secure.
Long may the elephant endure!

Arnold Sundgaard

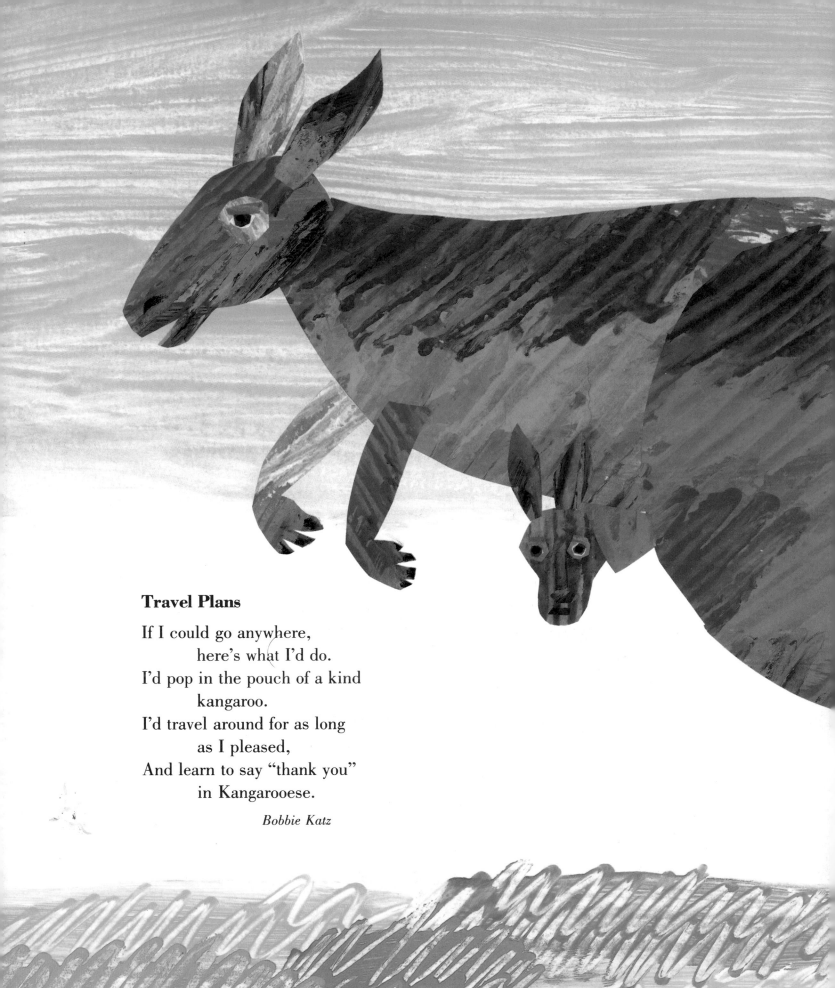

Travel Plans

If I could go anywhere,
    here's what I'd do.
I'd pop in the pouch of a kind
    kangaroo.
I'd travel around for as long
    as I pleased,
And learn to say "thank you"
    in Kangarooese.

Bobbie Katz

Seal Lullaby

Oh! hush thee, my baby, the night is behind us.
    And black are the waters that sparkled so green.
The moon, o'er the combers, looks downward to find us
    At rest in the hollows that rustle between.
Where billow meets billow, there soft be thy pillow;
    Ah, weary wee flipperling, curl at thy ease!
The storm shall not wake thee, no shark overtake thee.
    Asleep in the arms of the slow-swinging seas.

Rudyard Kipling

The Tortoise and the Hedgehog

Can't curl, but can swim—
Slow-Solid, that's him!
Curls up, but can't swim—
Stickly-Prickly, that's him.

Rudyard Kipling

Busy

Busy, busy, busy, busy,
Busy little squirrel—
Running, running, jumping,
In a dizzy whirl.
Stopping now and then to eat
A tasty little acorn treat—
Busy, busy, busy, busy,
Busy little squirrel.

Phyllis Halloran

Butterfly

What is a butterfly? At best
He's but a caterpillar dressed.

Benjamin Franklin

How Doth the Little Crocodile

How doth the little crocodile
   Improve his shining tail,
And pour the waters of the Nile
   On every golden scale!

How cheerfully he seems to grin,
   How neatly spreads his claws,
And welcomes little fishes in,
   With greatly smiling jaws!

Lewis Carroll

The Duck

Behold the duck.
It does not cluck.
A cluck it lacks.
It quacks.
It is especially fond
Of a puddle or pond.
When it dines or sups,
It bottoms up.

Ogden Nash

Long Gone

Don't waste your time in looking for
the long-extinct tyrannosaur,
because this ancient dinosaur
just can't be found here anymore.

This also goes for stegosaurus,
allosaurus, brontosaurus
and any other kind of saurus.
They all lived here before us.

Jack Prelutsky

The Lizard

The Lizard is a timid thing
That cannot dance or fly or sing;
He hunts for bugs beneath the floor
And longs to be a dinosaur.

John Gardner

Five little owls in the old elm tree
Fluffy and puffy as owls could be,
Blinking and winking with big round eyes
At the big round moon that hung in the skies.
As I passed beneath, I could hear one say,
"There'll be mouse for supper, there will today."
Then all of them hooted "Tu-whit, Tu-whoo!
Yes, mouse for supper, Hoo hoo. Hoo hoo!"

Anonymous

Firefly

A little light is going by,
Is going up to see the sky,
A little light with wings.

I never could have thought of it,
To have a little bug all lit
And made to go on wings.

Elizabeth Madox Roberts

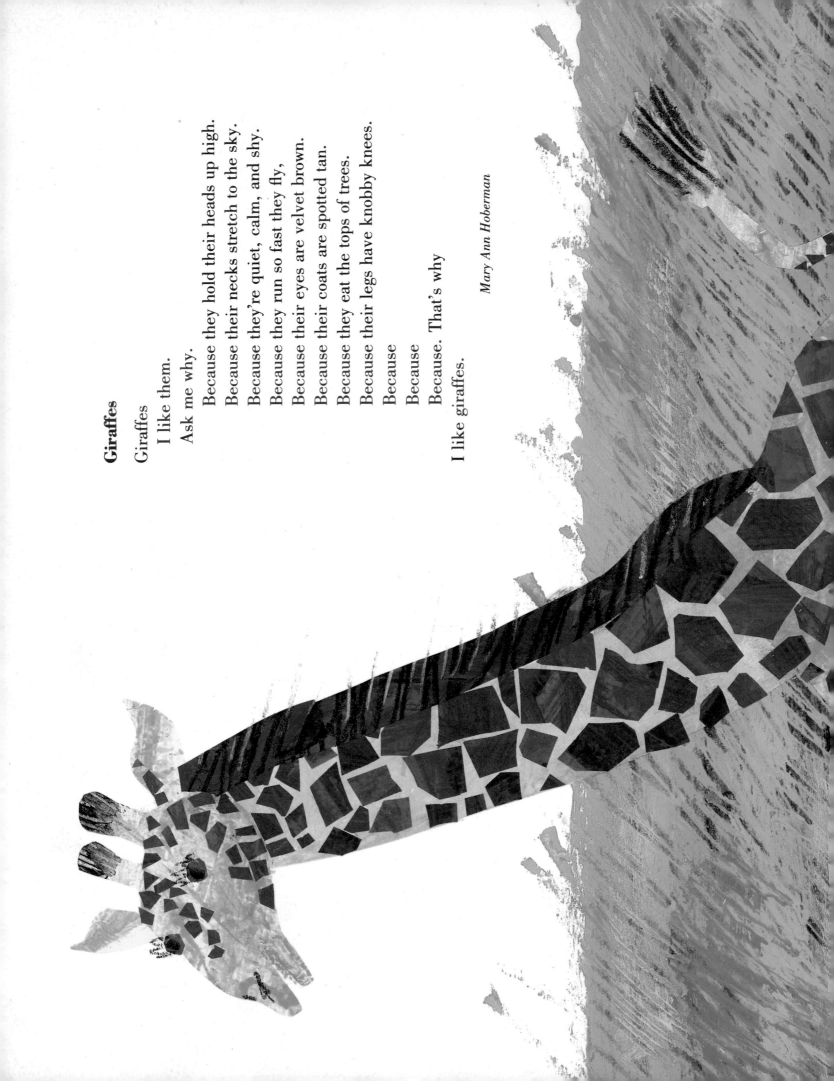

Giraffes

Giraffes
  I like them.
    Ask me why.
      Because they hold their heads up high.
      Because their necks stretch to the sky.
      Because they're quiet, calm, and shy.
      Because they run so fast they fly,
      Because their eyes are velvet brown.
      Because their coats are spotted tan.
      Because they eat the tops of trees.
      Because their legs have knobby knees.
      Because
      Because
      Because. That's why
    I like giraffes.

Mary Ann Hoberman

"Quack!" Said the Billy Goat

"Quack!" said the billy goat,
    "Oink!" said the hen.
"Miaow!" said the little chick
    Running in the pen.

"Hobble-gobble!" said the dog,
    "Cluck!" said the sow.
"Tu-whit-tu-whoo!" the donkey said,
    "Baa!" said the cow.

"Hee-haw!" the turkey cried,
    The duck began to moo.
All at once the sheep went,
    "Cock-a-doodle-doo!"
"Bleat! Bleat!" said the owl
    When he began to speak.
"Bow-wow!" said the cock
    Swimming in the creek.

"Cheep-cheep!" said the cat
    As she began to fly.
"Farmer's been and laid an egg—
    That's the reason why."

Charles Causley

50

If a rooster crows when he goes to bed
He'll get up with rain on his head.

Weather saying

When a peacock loudly calls
Then look out for rain and squalls.

Weather saying

What fun   to be
A Hippo   -potamus
And weigh   a ton
From top   to bottamus.

Michael Flanders

The Porcupine

A porcupine looks somewhat silly.
He also is extremely quilly.
And if he shoots a quill at you,
Run fast
Or you'll be quilly too.

I would not want a porcupine
To be my loving valentine.

Karla Kuskin

58

Mother Doesn't Want a Dog

Mother doesn't want a dog.
Mother says they smell,
And never sit when you say sit
Or even when you yell.
And when you come home late at night,
And there is ice and snow,
You have to go back out because
The dumb dog has to go.

Mother doesn't want a dog.
Mother says they shed,
And always let the strangers in
And bark at friends instead.
And do disgraceful things on rugs,
And track mud on the floor,
And flop upon your bed at night
And snore their doggy snore.

Mother doesn't want a dog.
She's making a mistake.
Because, more than a dog, I think
She will not want this snake.

Judith Viorst

The Flying Squirrel

The Flying Squirrel is crazy.
Though he has no feathers (much less wings),
He scampers up into the tallest tree
And cries, "Toot-toot! I'm a parachute!"
And away off the highest branches he springs
Into empty air, spreading every hair,
His arms and legs spread wide to the side,
Till he lands with a thump that's almost quiet . . .

Admire it child, but don't try it.

John Gardner

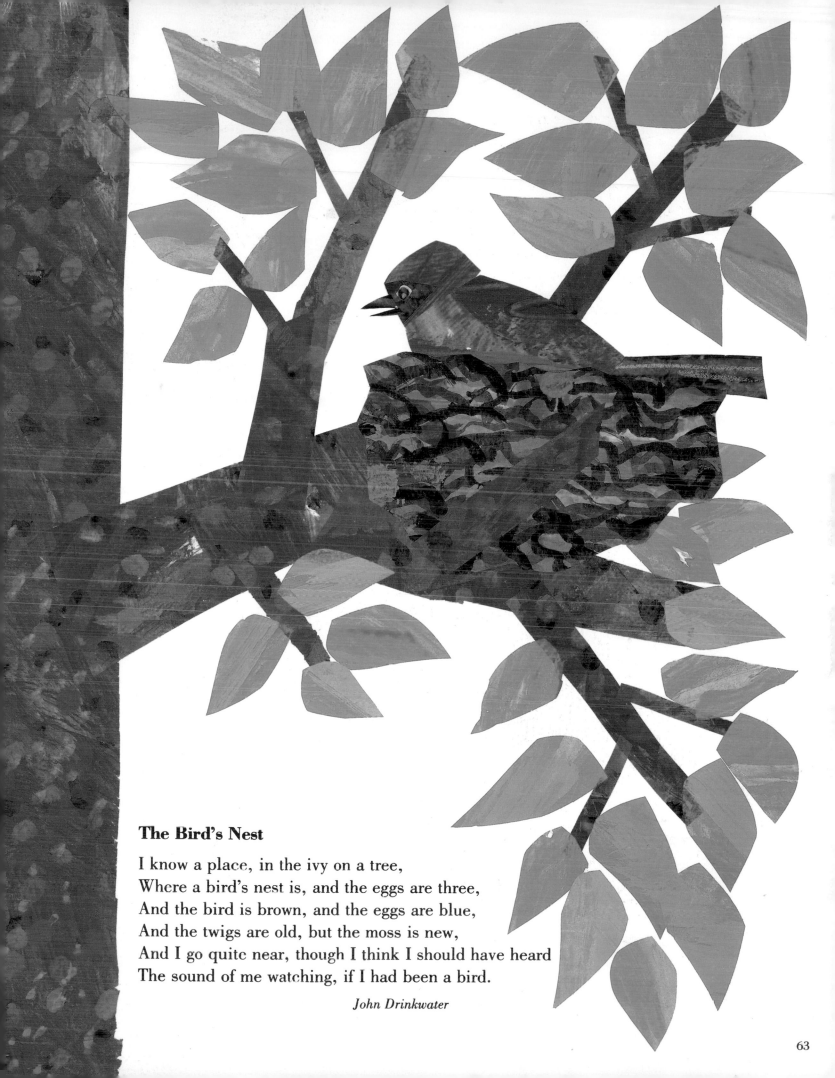

The Bird's Nest

I know a place, in the ivy on a tree,
Where a bird's nest is, and the eggs are three,
And the bird is brown, and the eggs are blue,
And the twigs are old, but the moss is new,
And I go quite near, though I think I should have heard
The sound of me watching, if I had been a bird.

John Drinkwater

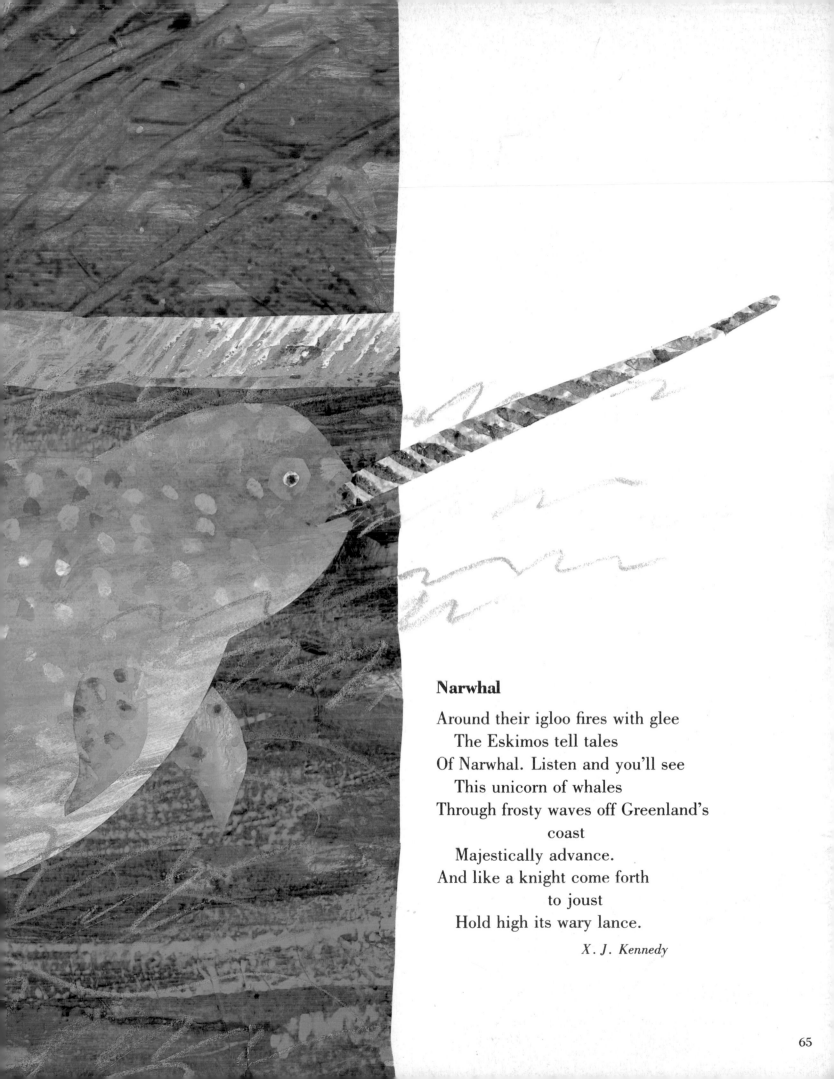

Narwhal

Around their igloo fires with glee
 The Eskimos tell tales
Of Narwhal. Listen and you'll see
 This unicorn of whales
Through frosty waves off Greenland's
  coast
 Majestically advance.
And like a knight come forth
  to joust
 Hold high its wary lance.

  X. J. Kennedy

Enigma Sartorial

Consider the Penguin.
He's smart as can be—
Dressed in his dinner clothes
Permanently.
You never can tell
When you see him about,
If he's just coming in
Or just going out!

Lucy W. Rhu

Yak

Yickity-yackity, yickity-yak,
the yak has a scriffily, scraffily back,
some yaks are brown yaks and some yaks are black,
yickity-yackity, yickity-yak.

Sniggildy-snaggildy, sniggildy-snag,
the yak is all covered with shiggildy-shag;
he walks with a ziggildy-zaggildy-zag,
sniggildy-snaggildy, sniggildy-snag.

Jack Prelutsky

The Pelican Chorus

King and Queen of the Pelicans we;
    No other birds so grand we see!
None but we have feet like fins!
With lovely, leathery throats and chins!
        Ploffskin, Pluffskin, Pelican jee!
        We think no birds as happy as we!
        Plumpskin, Plashkin, Pelican jill!
        We think so then, and we thought so still!

Edward Lear

Sparrow

A hummingbird hums.

A woodpecker drums.

A jay finds fighting
Pretty exciting
And licks every bird in sight.

A swallow swoops
In up-and-down loops
And seldom lights on the ground.

A gull is graceful in flight.

But take a sparrow
Whose world is narrow,
A sparrow just hangs around.

And an owl hoo-hoos
Whenever it gives a hoot.

A partridge whirs
Through the pines and the firs.

A chickadee's ways are cute.

A crow steals corn
From the year it's born
Then hides where it can't be found.

A sparrow, though,
Doesn't come and go,
A sparrow just hangs around.

Kaye Starbird

A pigeon coos

The Eagle

The sun's rays
Lie along my wings
And stretch beyond their tips.

Papago Indian

72

I will not change my horse with any that treads . . .
When I bestride him I soar. I am a hawk.
He trots the air; the earth sings when he touches it.

Shakespeare

Galloping pony—
alone, against the moonlight,
on a whitened beach.

Haiku, Kyorai

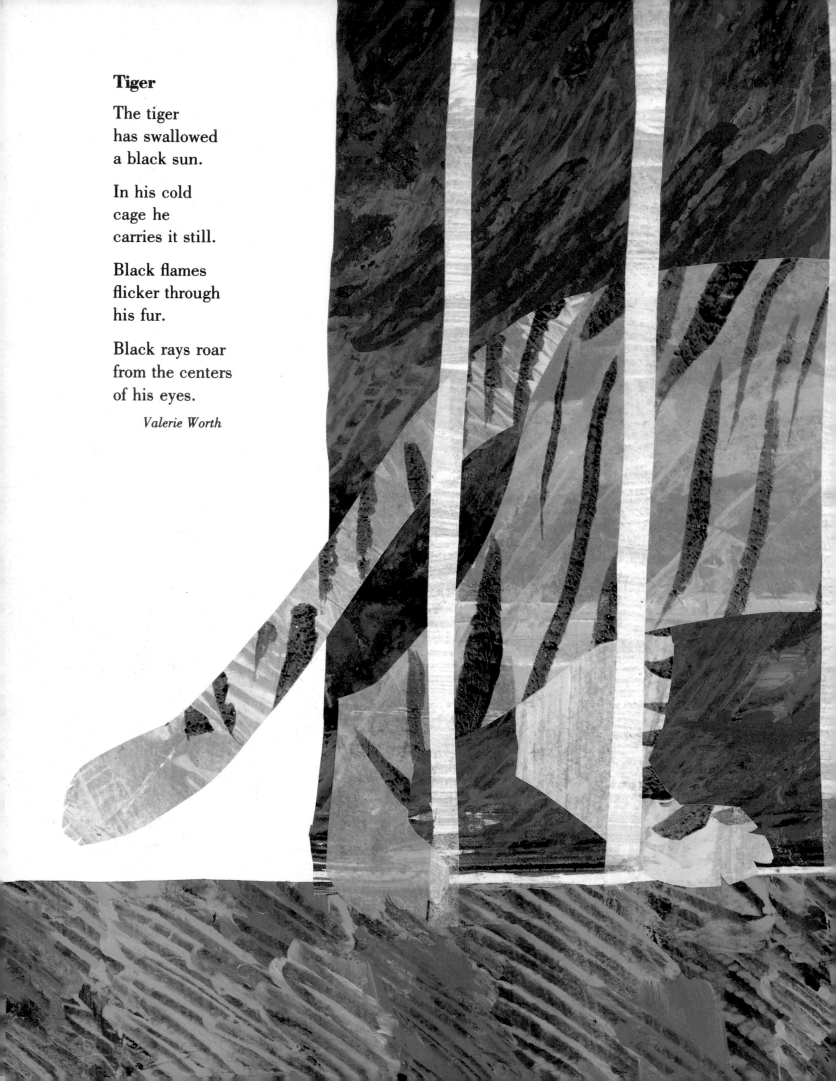

Tiger

The tiger
has swallowed
a black sun.

In his cold
cage he
carries it still.

Black flames
flicker through
his fur.

Black rays roar
from the centers
of his eyes.

Valerie Worth

The Barracuda

Slowly, slowly he cruises,
And slowly, slowly he chooses
Which kind of fish he prefers to take this morning;
Then without warning
The Barracuda opens his jaws, teeth flashing,
And with a horrible, horrible grinding and gnashing,
Devours a hundred poor creatures and feels no remorse.
It's no wonder of course,
That he really ought, perhaps, to change his ways.
"But" (as he says
With an evil grin)
"It's actually not my fault, you see!
I've nothing to do with the tragedy;
I open my mouth for a yawn and—ah me—
They all
       swim
          in."

John Gardner

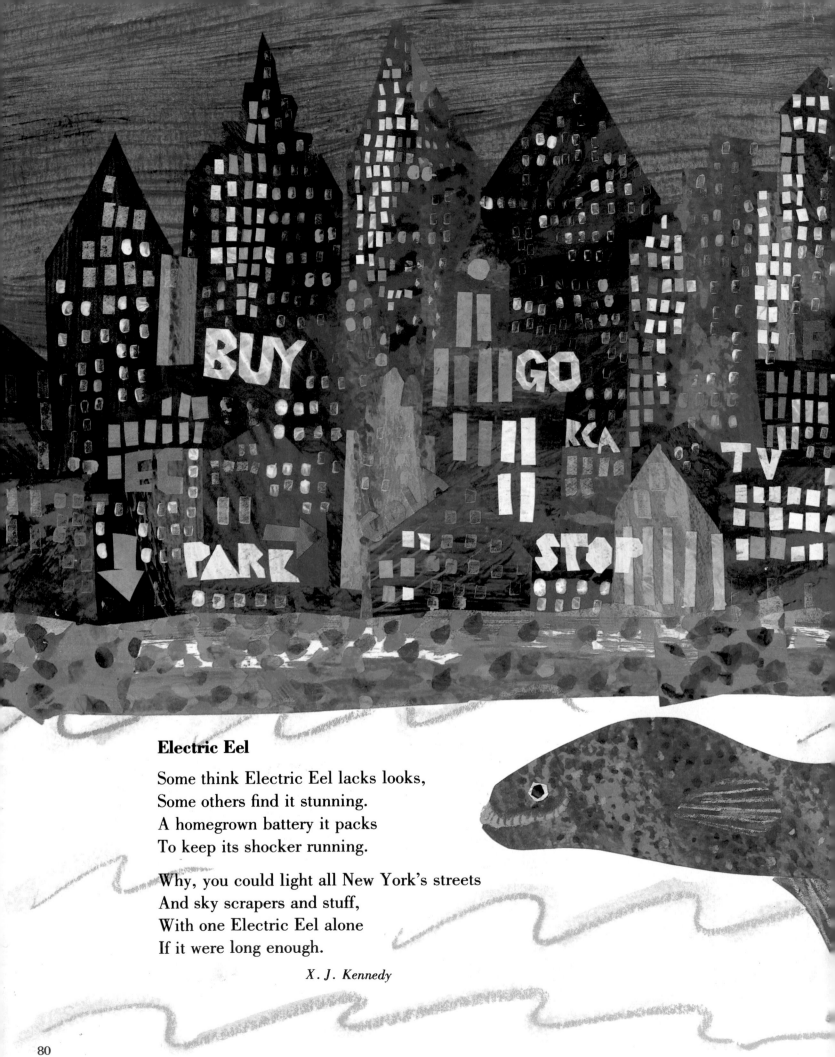

Electric Eel

Some think Electric Eel lacks looks,
Some others find it stunning.
A homegrown battery it packs
To keep its shocker running.

Why, you could light all New York's streets
And sky scrapers and stuff,
With one Electric Eel alone
If it were long enough.

X. J. Kennedy

80

The face of the dragonfly
Is practically nothing
But eyes.

Haiku, Chisoku

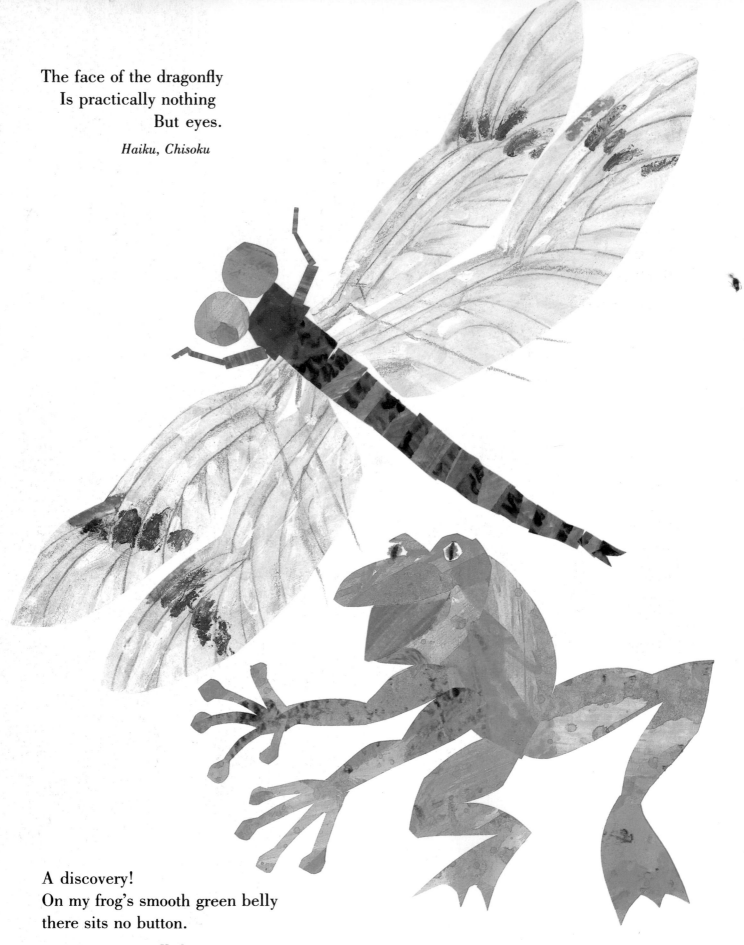

A discovery!
On my frog's smooth green belly
there sits no button.

Haiku, Yaku

Snail

Snail upon the wall,
Have you got at all
Anything to tell
About your shell?

Only this, my child—
When the wind is wild,
Or when the sun is hot,
It's all I've got.

John Drinkwater

Roosters

"Get out of my way!"
   says Rooster One.
"I won't!"
   says Rooster Two.
"You won't?"
"I won't!"
"You shall!"
"I shan't!"
Cock cock-a-
doodle-doo.
They picked.
They kicked.
They fought for hours.
There was a great
to-do!
"You're a very fine fighter,"
   says Rooster One.
"You're right!"
   says Rooster Two.

Elizabeth Coatsworth

The Red Hen

She turned her head to this side;
　　She turned her head to that.
Looking round for tidbits,
　　Juicy ones and fat.

Scritchy-scratch went Red Hen's feet;
　　Nib-nob went her bill.
She ate of juicy tidbits,
　　Until she had her fill.

And then she flew into a nest
　　And laid an egg, and then.
With a cut-cut-cut, ca-dah-cut,
　　Flew off to eat again.

James S. Tippett

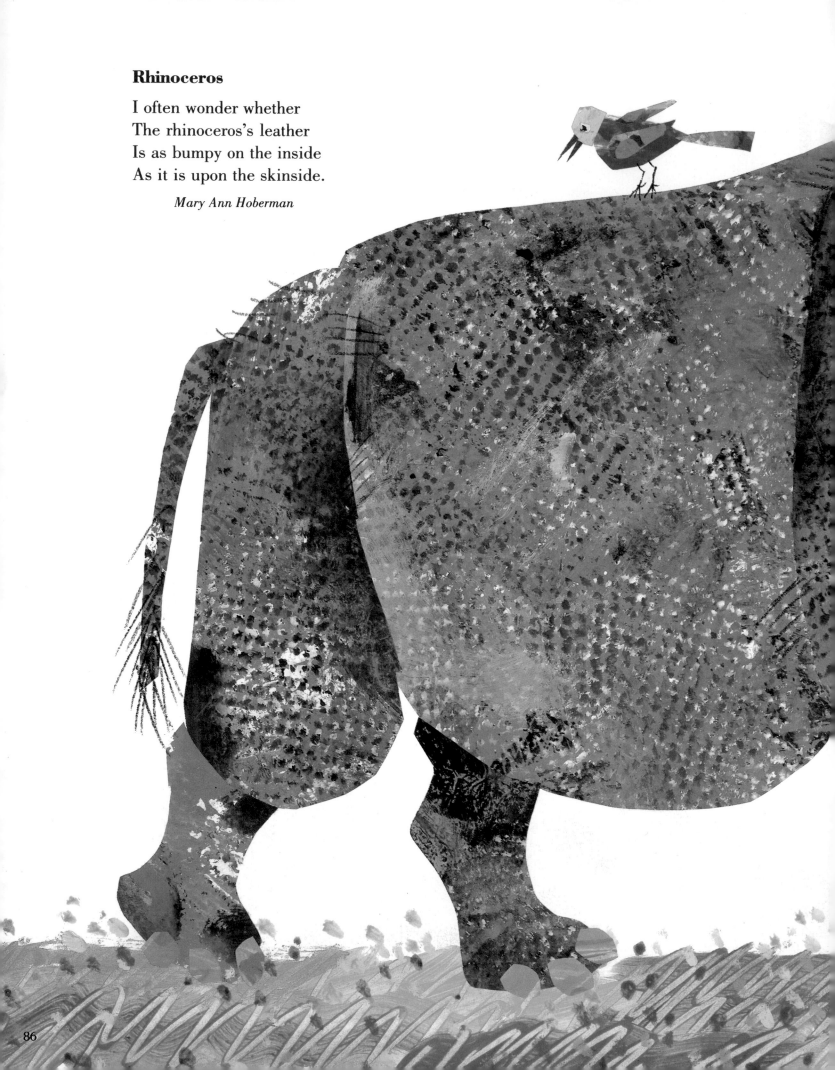

Rhinoceros

I often wonder whether
The rhinoceros's leather
Is as bumpy on the inside
As it is upon the skinside.

Mary Ann Hoberman

H

urt no living thing:
  Ladybird, nor butterfly,
Nor moth with dusty wing,
  Nor cricket chirping cheerily,
Nor grasshopper so light of leap.
  Nor dancing gnat, or beetle flat,
Nor harmless worms that creep.

Christina Rossetti

Index of Animals Alphabetically Arranged

Index of First Lines

Copyright Acknowledgements

Grateful acknowledgement is made to the following for permission to reprint from previously published material. Every effort has been made to trace owners of copyright in the material in this book. The Publishers apologise for any omission of which they would appreciate being informed so that due acknowledgement may be made in future impressions.

Dorothy Aldis: 'Every Insect' by Dorothy Aldis reprinted by permission of G. P. Putnam's Sons from *Quick as a Wink*, by Dorothy Aldis. Copyright © 1960 Dorothy Aldis, copyright renewed © 1988 by Roy E. Porter.

Harry Behn: 'Crickets', from *Crickets and Bullfrogs and Whispers of Thunder*, poems and pictures by Harry Behn, edited by Lee Bennett Hopkins. Copyright 1949, 1953, © 1956, 1957, 1966, 1968 by Harry Behn. Copyright renewed © 1981 by Alice Behn Goebel, Pamela Behn Adam, Prescott Behn and Peter Behn. Reprinted by permission of Marian Reiner.

Charles Causley: 'Quack! Said the Billy Goat', from *Figgie Hobbin*, by Charles Causley, published by Macmillan. Reprinted by permission of David Higham Associates Limited.

Elizabeth Coatsworth: 'Roosters', from *Poems* by Elizabeth Coatsworth. Reprinted with the permission of the Estate of Elizabeth Coatsworth by arrangement with Mark Paterson & Associates.

John Drinkwater: 'Snail' and 'The Bird's Nest' by John Drinkwater. Reprinted with the permission of the Estate of John Drinkwater and Samuel French Limited.

Aileen Fisher: 'Baby Chick', from *Runny Days, Sunny Days*, by Aileen Fisher. Copyright © 1958 by Aileen Fisher. Copyright renewed © 1986 by Aileen Fisher. Reprinted by permission of the author.

John Gardner: 'The Flying Squirrel', 'The Barracuda', and 'The Lizard', from *A Child's Bestiary*, by John Gardner. Copyright © 1977 by Boskydell Artists, Ltd. Reprinted by permission of Georges Borchardt Inc.

Phyllis Halloran: 'Busy' and 'Patience', by Phyllis Halloran. Copyright © 1989 by Phyllis Halloran. Reprinted by the permission of the author.

Bobbi Katz: 'Travel Plans', from *Upside Down and Inside Out* by Bobbi Katz. Copyright © 1973 by Bobbi Katz. Reprinted by permission of the author.

X.J. Kennedy: 'Electric Eel' and 'Narwhal', from *Adam Did Name the Vinegarroon*, by X.J. Kennedy. Copyright © 1982 by X.J. Kennedy. Reprinted by permission of David R. Godine, Publisher.

Karla Kuskin: 'The Porcupine', from *Cricket Magazine*. Copyright © 1974 by Karla Kuskin. Reprinted by permission of the author.

Richard Lewis: 'The Eagle' (Papago), 'I Throw Myself to the Left!' (African Pygmy), and 'Sea Turtle' (Australian Aborigine), from *Out of the Earth I Sign*, edited by Richard Lewis. Copyright © 1968 by Richard Lewis. Reprinted by permission of Grosset & Dunlap, Inc.

Eve Merriam: 'The Birthday Cow', from *The Birthday Cow*, by Eve Merriam. Copyright © 1978 by Eve Merriam. Reprinted by permission of Marian Reiner for the author.

Ogden Nash: 'The Octopus', from *Verses from 1929 On*, by Ogden Nash. Copyright 1942 by Ogden Nash. First appeared in *The New Yorker*. 'The Duck', from *Verses from 1929 On*, by Ogden Nash. Copyright 1936 by Ogden Nash. First appeared in *The Saturday Evening Post*. Reprinted by kind permission of Curtis Brown, London, on behalf of the Estate of Ogden Nash.

Jack Prelutsky: 'Yak' and 'Long Gone' from *Zoo Doings*, by Jack Prelutsky. Copyright © 1983 by Jack Prelutsky. Reprinted by permission of Greenwillow Books, a division of William Morrow & Co.

Lucy Rhu: 'Enigma Sartorial', by Lucy Rhu, from *The Barnes Book of Nursery Verse*, by Barbara Ireson. Published by A.S. Barnes.

Carl Sandburg: Last verse of 'Timesweep', originally from 'Names' in *Wind Song*. Copyright 1953 by Carl Sandburg and renewed 1981 by Margaret Sandburg, Janet Sandburg, and Helga Sandburg Crile, reprinted by permission of Harcourt Brace Jovanovich, Inc.

Arnold Sundgaard: 'The Duck-Billed Platypus' and 'The Elephant', by Arnold Sundgaard. Copyright © 1989 by Arnold Sundgaard. Reprinted by permission of the author.

Judith Viorst: 'Mother Doesn't Want a Dog', from *If I Were in Charge of the World and Other Worries*, by Judith Viorst. Copyright © 1981 by Judith Viorst. Reprinted with the permission of Lescher and Lescher.

Valerie Worth: 'Tiger' from *Small Poems Again* by Valerie Worth. Copyright © 1975, 1986 by Valerie Worth. Reprinted by permission of Farrar, Straus & Giroux, Inc.

Eric Carle prepares his own coloured tissue papers. Different textures are achieved by using various brushes to splash, splatter and finger-paint acrylic paints on to thin tissue papers. These coloured tissue papers then become his palette. They are cut or torn into shapes as needed and are glued on to white illustration board. Some areas of his design, however, are painted directly on the board before the bits of tissue paper are applied to make the collage illustration.

Laura Whipple, who collected the poems for this special anthology, is an elementary school media specialist and a graduate of Rutgers University Graduate School of Communication, Information, and Library Studies, in the USA.

British Library Cataloguing in Publication Data

Carle, Eric, *1929–*
Eric Carle's animals animals.
1. Children's literature in English. Special Subjects: Animals – Anthologies
I. Title   II. Whipple, Laura
820.8036

ISBN 0-340-50120-0

First published by 1989 by Philomel Books, New York, USA
First published in Great Britain 1990

Published by Hodder and Stoughton Children's Books,
a division of Hodder and Stoughton Ltd,
Mill Road, Dunton Green, Sevenoaks, Kent TN13 2YA

Printed in Belgium by Proost International Book Production